MOUSEKIN'S MYSTERY

Story and pictures by

EDNA MILLER

Prentice-Hall, Inc., *Englewood Cliffs, N.J.*

For Ruth and Joe Jackson Jr.

Printed in the United States of America   ·J

Prentice-Hall International, Inc., London
Prentice-Hall of Australia, Pty. Ltd., Sydney
Prentice-Hall of Canada, Inc., Toronto
Prentice-Hall of India Private Ltd., New Delhi
Prentice-Hall of Japan, Inc., Tokyo
Prentice-Hall of Southeast Asia Pte. Ltd., Singapore
Whitehall Books Limited, Wellington, New Zealand
Editora Prentice-Hall Do Brasil LTDA., Rio de Janeiro

10 9 8 7 6 5 4 3 2 1

Library of Congress Cataloging in Publication Data

Miller, Edna.
  Mousekin's mystery.

  Summary: After his home is burned by lightning during
a summer storm, Mousekin is frightened by a strange pale
light in the dark forest which he eventually learns to
be fox fire, a glow caused by fungi in decaying wood.
  [1. Mice–Fiction.   2. Mystery and detective stories.
3. Bioluminescence–Fiction]   I. Title.
PZ7.M6128Mp 1983   [E]   83-9622
ISBN 0-13-604330-5

There are firefly lights in a summer woods
that wink and blink in the dark.
There are mushrooms that light the forest floor
and shine with a cool, steady glow.
Some mushrooms that grow on rotting wood
give out a ghostly light.
When animals brush this "living light,"
their coats will gleam.
But Mousekin didn't know this...

Lightning had struck Mousekin's hollow-tree home
while he was away in the storm.
Now all that was left was the trunk of the tree.
It glowed bright red inside.

The heat of the dying embers
made Mousekin jump away,
and the heavy smoke that filled the air
made his silky whiskers tremble.

Mousekin darted into the woods
to find some other shelter
from owls and furry creatures
who hunt for mice at night.

While he stopped for a moment
to poke through leaves
for a mouse-size opening,
he heard a grunting sound.

Mousekin spun around to see
something moving through the trees
in the dark and misty woods.

It ambled slowly toward him.
It glowed with a pale blue light.

Mousekin scrambled to the top of a tree
and hid amongst its branches.
From his high safe perch he peeked to see
a ghostly bear below him...
gleaming in the dark.

The creature growled softly,
then wandered away,
back into a thicket of trees.

As Mousekin sniffed the air for smoke
and peered about for fire,
another creature with an eerie glow
glided by him in the dark.

He watched the flying squirrel
disappear in branches below.
Its shining underbody lit
the trunk of the tree where it landed.

Mousekin tightened his hold on the branch
when a fox padded silently by.
Only its head and its long bushy tail
glistened in the night.
Mousekin shuddered when he heard
yaps and squeals below.
The ghostly fox, with its shining head,
sent a creature up into the tree.

A young raccoon with a glowing mask
saw Mousekin race to the ground.

Mousekin ran as fast as he could
from that haunted place in the forest.
He ran through the woods 'til morning light
touched the top of the trees.

Too tired to find a safer bed,
he crept under a bit of moss.
Curling up into a furry ball,
he slept 'til the sun was high.

It isn't safe for a white-footed mouse
to be awake in the day,
but Mousekin was hungry when he awoke.
There were berries and seeds nearby.
As he nibbled and gnawed he heard a grunt.
He had heard *that* sound before.

Mousekin crouched and looked to see
a bear...rolling about in a hollow log.
It grunted and growled with pleasure
as it scratched its shaggy back.
(The bear didn't glow in the daylight.)

When the bear wandered off,
there were others that came
to visit the hollow log.
A fox leaped in and spun about
to catch a tiny shrew.
(The fox didn't glow in the daylight.)

A raccoon pawed through the rotting wood
for things that creep and crawl.
(The raccoon didn't glow in the daylight.)

At twilight a flying squirrel landed
in the middle of the log.
It searched for acorns in a litter of leaves.
(The squirrel didn't glow in the twilight.)

When the squirrel scampered away
and the forest grew still,
Mousekin hid near the fallen log
and slept 'til evening came.
As the sky grew darker and darker,
the mysterious light lit the woods.
Mousekin awakened with a start.

Before him was the moss-covered log.
It was bathed in a brilliant blue light.
There was no smoke. There was no heat...
as when lightning had struck his home!
Mousekin crept close to the fallen log.
Its glow was as cool as firefly light.

While Mousekin circled the shining log,
a young owl swooped for its prey.

The white-footed mouse was quick
to dive inside the fallen tree.
He burrowed deep within its spongy layers.
In every crack and crevice
there were threads of "living light"...
glowing mushroom feeders that live on rotting wood.

Mousekin waited 'til it was safe
to peek around outside.

As Mousekin raced to a sturdy oak tree,
the frightened young owl flew away.
It had never seen a white-footed mouse
gleam in the dark before!

On a branch of the tree, near a snug new home,
Mousekin cleaned his furry coat.
The tasteless, scentless mushroom glow
was quick to disappear.

Mousekin knew now that there were no ghosts
prowling about in the forest...
there were only natural living lights
that blink or glow in the dark.